The Lives of Lemurs

An Unnatural History

ANDREA ANTINORI

T tra.publishing

Dear Reader,

This book provides an in-depth look at the history and social behavior of lemurs. It starts with their arrival in Madagascar and then explores their habits and ways. This work is the result of extensive research, carried out both at a distance and in direct contact with lemurs.

But the purely scientific part is not the whole story. This book blends factual information with creativity and imagination, resulting in another kind of story. I would like to be clear that it's not all fake, but it's not all true, either. Not exactly.

I apologize to any readers who thought this book was a genuine study on natural history. I suggest that you keep reading, because you will have fun, and you will learn about lemurs. And don't miss the back section, which does have lots of real facts!

Enjoy!

Here they are, the lemurs.

They are prosimians belonging to the order Primates. If you want to be more general, they are also mammals.

I guess they're kind of like us. You could almost say that they are our early ancestors, with the difference being that we can still find them here on Earth!

bamboo lemur

aye-aye

indri

sifaka

But where on Earth?

Well, lemurs are unique in that they live only in Madagascar. But that wasn't always the case: they used to live in Africa, on the mainland.

ring-tailed lemur

red ruffed lemur

They got along well with monkeys.

But the problem was that the monkey population

kept on growing, and growing, and growing.

So the lemurs decided to leave for the
island of Madagascar.

But there was a problem.

The sea.

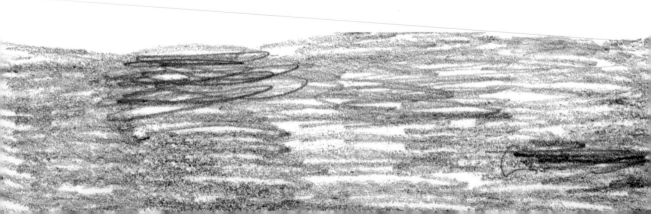

To make the great crossing, the lemurs used many techniques.

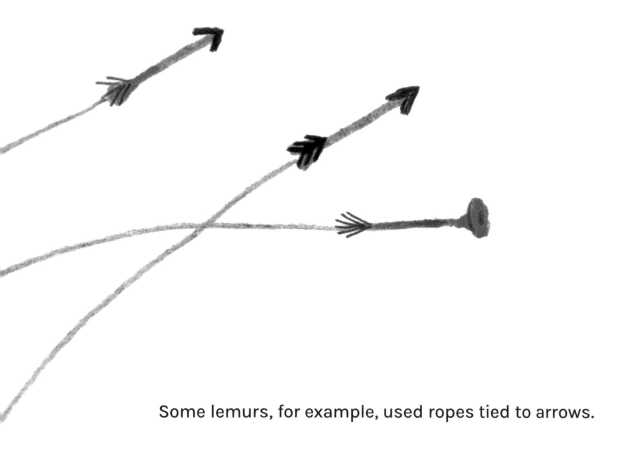

Some lemurs, for example, used ropes tied to arrows.

Once they hooked onto the island with the arrows,
it was a piece of cake to cross the sea.

Other lemurs migrated aboard a sperm whale.

But the fearless ones got there by clinging

to branches, logs, and other pieces of wood.

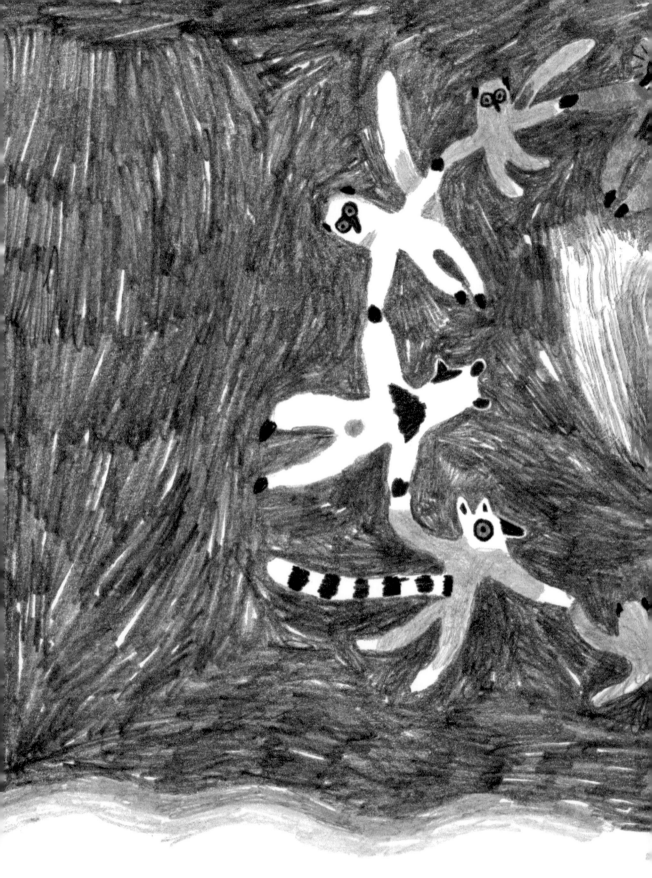

Once they got to Madagascar,

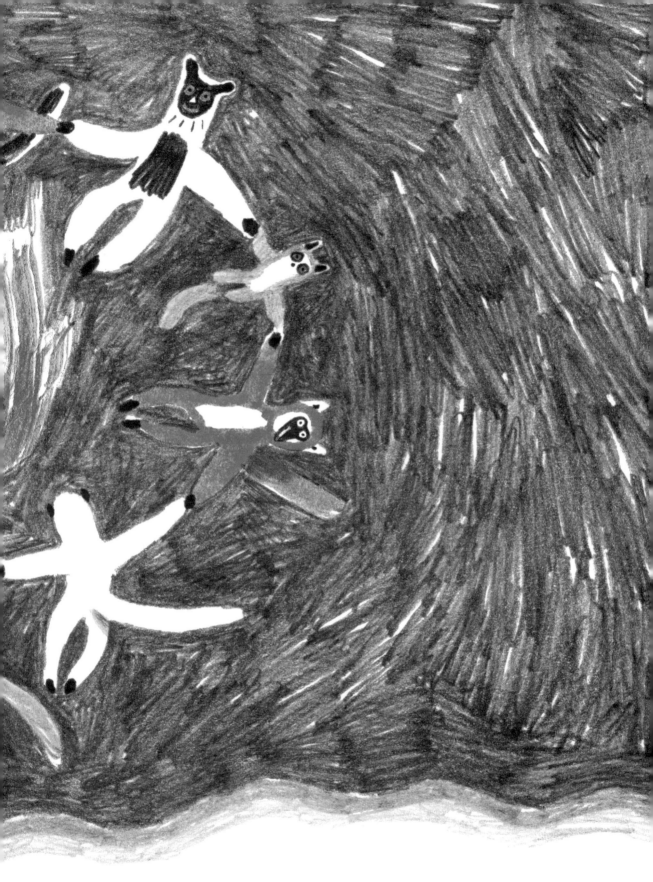

the lemurs did the sifaka dance in a circle.

There were no other animals in Madagascar at that time, but luckily lemurs are vegetarians.

They are especially fond of fruit. Each lemur has his or her own preferences of what to eat.

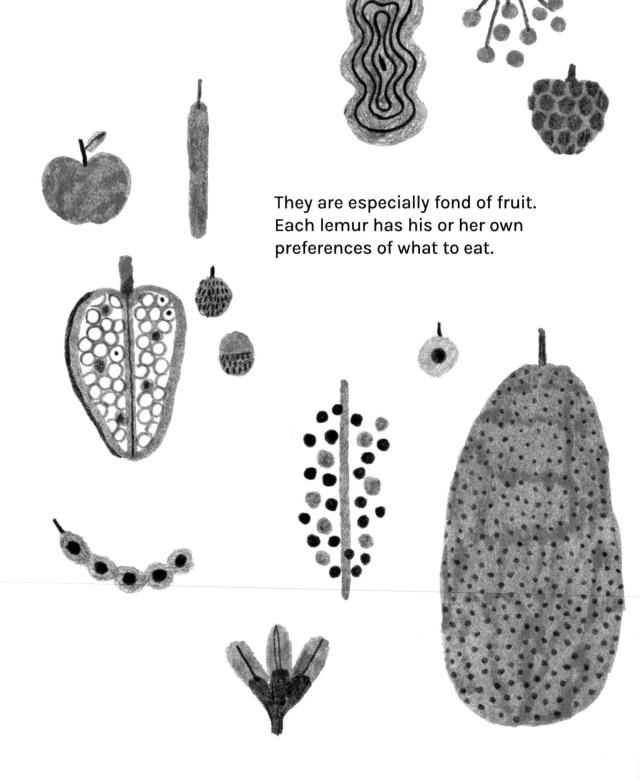

The females get the best fruit.

The males have to make do
with whatever fruit is left over.

Lemurs also have a deity, the giant ball.
And it is exactly that—a giant ball that
floats in the middle of the sky.

The lemurs worship it in a meditative stance.

The most dedicated
even manage to levitate.

They worship the giant ball because
it makes the fruit grow,

and because it dries them out after the rain.

Life in Madagascar was quiet at first.
No one bothered the lemurs, and most
importantly, no one tried to eat them.
And that stayed true until the arrival
of the fossa.

Since then, lemurs have lived
as high up as possible.
And even there, each one
has his or her own personal
preferences.

High in the trees, lemurs dabble in a variety of activities. There are some who like to play instruments,

others sing,

and most lemurs have a great passion
for cooking (and eating).

Certain lemurs, on the other hand, pass their time maintaining hygiene and cleanliness.

And while some sleep, the aye-ayes
stay awake and count the stars.

All in all, even with the fossa there, Madagascar remained a quiet land for the lemurs, where peaceful coexistence (and competition) prevailed.

That was until monkeys, who were
much bigger than lemurs, moved in.

They began to take over vast spaces,
build huge burrows, and knock down trees.

Since that time, lemurs stopped feeling
safe, and they started hiding.

But all is not lost.

When you set off to explore Madagascar,
be very aware.

Keep your eyes and ears open,
yout chin up, and don't make a sound.

The lemurs are everywhere,
and they are watching you!

Real Information

There are over one hundred species of lemurs...they are native to Madagascar, an island off the coast of Africa...they are among the most endangered group of mammals on the planet...and lots more actual facts.

Madagascar: The Island Where the Lemurs Live

Madagascar is the fourth largest island in the world. It is located in the Indian Ocean about 260 miles east of the southeast coast of Africa. Madagascar is an island nation, meaning that it is its own country. It is 228,900 square miles, which is a little larger than the country of France and almost as big as the state of Texas.

Rainforest

Spiny thicket

Temperate deciduous forest

Madagascar is the only place in the world where the lemurs live.

Geologically, the land that is Madagascar was once part of the same continent as Africa and India.

Madagascar moved away from the mainland of Africa about 160 million years ago, and then split from the Indian tectonic plate around eighty million years ago.

That long isolation from other land masses is why there are many animals and plants that are unique to the island. In fact, about ninety-five percent of the island's reptiles, eighty-nine percent of its plant life, and ninety-two percent of its mammals are endemic, meaning they are only found there.

The ancestors of present-day lemurs were in Madagascar about fifty million years ago. The absence of other primates limited interspecies competition for food and territory, allowing lemurs to evolve in peace. Those ancient animals diversified into more than one hundred species and subspecies today.

We don't know how the primeval lemurs arrived in Madagascar. Some scientists think that they made their way across the ocean on makeshift rafts, such as floating logs.

Other scientists believe that lemurs were already on the land and were "trapped" there once the island detached.

The first human beings arrived in Madagascar about two thousand years ago from present-day Indonesia. This is a journey stretching more than thirty-five hundred miles (that is about the same length as the east coast to the west coast of the United States). Archaeologists believe that the humans traveled by canoe and came in multiple groups over hundreds of years.

Madagascar varies greatly in climate and environment. The eastern part of the island has a hot and humid climate and is covered by rainforest, while the south has a dry climate, perfect for the spiny thicket. There is a large plateau in the center of the island. The northwestern area has a dry and temperate climate, with deciduous forests; it is there that you can find the baobab trees, which Madagascar is famous for.

Each environment is home to different lemurs, which have adapted to the specific type of climate and vegetation.

Lemurs are primates, which means they belong to the same group of mammals as apes, monkeys, and humans. They began to diversify from an ancestral primate about sixty million years ago, taking a different evolutionary course. They are prosimians, a word that means "before the apes," and they have retained many characteristics from their ancestral primates. Today, we are aware of more than one hundred species of lemurs. One of the unique aspects of lemurs is that they are native to Madagascar—it is only on this island that they can be found in the wild. They are also the only primates that live in Madagascar (except for humans).

The sifaka dance is a simple way of moving around on the ground. In fact, sifaka are mainly arboreal lemurs, which means they live in trees. They leap from tree to tree, often leaping more than twenty feet. When they move on the ground, they jump around using the power in their lower limbs while moving their forelimbs to allow them to balance their body.

Lemurs tend to eat a fruit-based diet. However, this varies depending on the species. For example, some lemurs are mostly herbivores, feeding on leaves and vegetation, while other species also eat larvae and insects. The evolutionary process has led animals to choose different food sources, limiting competition between species. Even among lemurs, the selection of certain plants or fruits is often very specific.

There are lemurs of many shapes and sizes. There are tiny lemurs, such as the Madame Berthe's mouse lemur, so small that they can fit into a little coffee cup. They weigh only one ounce, winning the title of the world's smallest primate. The indri is the largest of the lemurs at about three feet tall and as heavy as sixty-five pounds. But in the past, there were even giant lemurs such as the Megaladapis, or koala lemur, which was the size of a chimpanzee.

In contrast to most other primates, certain species of lemurs live in matriarchal societies where it is the females who have a dominant position over the males. For instance, female ring-tailed lemurs have priority over food, they lead the group, and they are the first to be cleaned when it comes to grooming.

The calls of the indri, often choral, are so loud that you can hear them from more than a mile away. The reasons can be various: they "sing" to establish the boundaries of their own territory, to keep in touch with the other members of the group, or as an alarm to signal the presence of danger.

The fossa is the lemurs' main predator. Like lemurs, the fossa is native to Madagascar. It is a relative of the mongoose, and some people compare it to a small cougar. It is the largest land carnivore in Madagascar, reaching six feet in length from its head to the tip of its tail. Contrary to the story in this book, the fossa is also arboreal and can easily climb trees.

Grooming is a typical behaviour for lemurs, and in general for all primates (except humans, which are the only primate species with mostly naked skin). It concerns the cleaning of fur carried out by one animal for another. This practice not only has a hygienic value, but also a social value by strengthening or repairing relationships between individuals, actually becoming a kind of "exchange currency."

Bamboo lemurs got their name because they feed mostly on bamboo. The plant contains the poison cyanide, which can kill other animals of the same size, but the bamboo lemur is immune to the poison. Instead, for them feeding on bamboo is a survival strategy.

The aye-aye is a nocturnal lemur. It has a unique feature: it has a particularly long and very thin middle finger, which it uses to find and extract the larvae living inside tree trunks. Unfortunately, its survival is severely strained due not only to environmental problems but also due to human superstitions.

Lemurs are arboreal, which means they live mainly in trees, and their type varies according to the local area and their diet. Among these, the ring-tailed lemurs are the ones that, compared with all the other species, lead a slightly more land-based life.

Many diurnal lemurs start the day by sunning: they sunbathe in a position that resembles a yoga pose. Lemurs are able to warm up in the early morning hours before starting their activities thanks to sunning. This practice has led some Malagasy people to think of lemurs as "sun worshippers."

Lemurs Are Endangered

As you've learned in this book, lemurs are amazing animals. They are also among the most endangered group of mammals on the planet. Of the more than one hundred species of lemurs, ninety-eight percent are endangered and thirty-one percent are critically endangered.

Why?

The two main reasons lemurs are endangered are deforestation and hunting. Unfortunately, both activities increased during the coronavirus pandemic, which put lemurs even more at risk than before.

Deforestation means a reduction in the forest (which is where lemurs live). This happens in Madagascar when people burn or cut down trees.

One reason that Malagasy people remove trees is to clear the land to plant crops. Hunger is a major issue in the country, and growing food is important to sustain the population. Another reason for deforestation is that some industries cut down trees so they can use the wood.

Lemur habitats are also threatened by the effects of climate change. Another main threat to the lemur population is that people hunt them for food. Beyond that, lemurs are also threatened by invasive species like stray cats and dogs.

What is being done to help the lemurs?

Fortunately, there are many wonderful organizations hard at work to help the lemurs by conserving the animals and their environment. These organizations protect the lemurs in various ways—mainly through scientific research, reforestation, establishing protected areas, relocation, breeding programs, education, and outreach.

Education helps!

Many people don't know a lot about lemurs, and they don't realize how endangered these animals are. People reading this book can help by learning more, telling others about lemurs, and researching ways to support lemurs. This is called raising awareness. The more people learn about lemurs, the more people can help.

Stories are a great way of spreading information. I dedicate this book to
Gerald Durrell, whose book *The Aye-aye and I: A Rescue Journey to Save
One of the World's Most Intriguing Creatures from Extinction* and his other books
are a constant inspiration for my work.—A.A.

We would like to thank the Parco Natura Viva for its scientific advice, in particular Cesare Avesani Zaborra, Katia Dell'Aira, Caterina Spiezio, and Marta Tezza. Many thanks also to Daniela Antonacci, Daniela Berti, and Noemi Vola.

Andrea Antinori is an award-winning illustrator based in Bologna, Italy. He has loved animals and loved to draw them since he was a kid. His favorite animal changes all the time. Right now he loves lemurs. Other books he has illustrated include *A Book About Whales* and *The Great Battle*, which has won major international awards. He studied graphic design and illustration at ISIA in Urbino and at Escola Massana in Barcelona.

Author & Illustrator
Andrea Antinori
Text and images © 2020 Andrea Antinori

Book Design
Andrea Antinori & corrainiStudio

U.S. Edition Publisher & Creative Director
Ilona Oppenheim

U.S. Edition Art Director
Jefferson Quintana

U.S. Edition Editor
Andrea Gollin

Printed and Bound in China
Shenzhen Reliance Printers

The Lives of Lemurs: An Unnatural History is printed on Forest Stewardship Council certified paper from well-managed forests.

MIX
Paper from responsible sources
FSC® C102842

Tra Publishing is committed to sustainability in its materials and practices.

Tra Publishing
245 NE 37th Street
Miami, FL 33137
trapublishing.com

T tra.publishing